A New Kind of Thanksgiving

T. Lawren

SC Luxury Publishing

To those who continue to pursue their dream, no matter the obstacle.

You matter, your work matters, and your dreams matter.

INSPIRATIONAL WORKBOOKS

Refining Your Life Through the Fire

The Path to Purpose Following the Principles of God: Reflection
Guide

INSPIRATIONAL

Dear Woman of God

The Path to Purpose Following the Principles of God

PLANNERS

Graced. Restored. Transformed.

ISBN: 979-8-9928077-3-8 (Paperback)

ISBN: 979-8-9928077-4-5 (ebook)

Library of Congress Control Number: 2025925589

Author name: T. Lawren, 1984

Published by: SC Luxury Publishing

Imprint: SC Luxury Publishing

Address:3195 Dowlen Rd, Ste 101-386 Beaumont, TX 77706

Website: www.tlawren.com

Chapter 1

The gavel's soft tap echoed through the council chamber, signaling the end of the meeting and the beginning of the part Malcolm Mouton liked the least–the lingering.

Rows of chairs scraped gently against the polished floor as people stood, stretching, buttoning coats, and gathering their folders. From his place at the front, Malcolm watched them move in twos and threes, voices rising in a low hum. The town's business was settled for the evening; budgets were approved, a minor zoning issue pushed to the next month, and the annual Eden's Harbour Thanksgiving Market formally green lit.

By all accounts, it had been a good night.

He adjusted his tie out of habit, fingers smoothing down the silk knot that hadn't moved. The motion gave him something to do with his hands while he prepared his ready made facial expressions that everyone expected to see on him, calm and approachable.

Mayor Mouton, their youngest elected leader. The man who never seemed rattled and always put together.

"Mayor, great job tonight."

He turned, offering the man who approached him, his rehearsed smile. "Thank you, Councilman Alvarado. Couldn't have done it without everyone's input."

Alvarado clasped his shoulder in a brief, friendly squeeze. "Folks will be happy. You know how they are about that market. Thanksgiving doesn't start until those tents go up."

"Don't I know it," Malcolm replied, chuckling on cue. "We'll make sure it's one for the books."

They exchanged a few more pleasantries about the vendor permits and weather forecasts, then Alvarado moved on, already halfway into a conversation with someone else. Malcolm's laughter faded as quickly as it had come, his face relaxing back into something closer to neutral. The room buzzed with little knots of conversation, agreements, and shared relief that another meeting was done.

To anyone watching, he looked like part of it.

Inside, he felt like he was standing behind glass.

He gathered his papers into a neat stack, even though his assistant would likely reorganize them in the morning. His movements were automatic now—straighten the pile, tuck it into the leather portfolio, cap the pen, slide into the case. Order in his hands, even if there wasn't much of it anywhere else.

"Mayor!"

He glanced up, smile already lifting before he saw who it was.

Mrs. Ramirez, owner of the floral shop on Maple, waved as she hurried down the aisle toward him. "I just had to say, that bit about making room in the budget for the veterans' luncheon?" She pressed a hand to her chest. "That meant a lot. My brother..." Her voice softened, and she shook her head. "Anyway. Thank you."

"You're welcome," he said gently. "It's the least we can do."

She lingered a second too long, her eyes flicking past his smile to search something in his face. He knew that look. He'd been catching it more often over the last two years, ever since the seat beside him at these meetings, stopped being *hers*. It was one of people wanting to say more, ask more, offer more, even pitying him.

People used to come up in pairs, glancing between him and the woman who could gently rescue him the moment conversations dragged on too long. She'd loop her arm through his, laugh softly, and say, *"Alright folks, last question before I steal my husband away."* Now people only looked at him...and the emptiness next to him.

Before she could reach for it, he gave her another warm, practiced nod. "Tell your brother I said hello."

"I will," she said, though the look remained. "Have a good night, Mayor."

"You too."

She left, and he exhaled slowly, the breath leaving his chest in a way that felt heavier than it should have.

Another cluster approached—two church deacons and a small business owner—ready to talk about streetlights and parking near the square. Malcolm shifted his shoulders back, slid the mayoral smile into place, and listened.

He answered their questions, reassuring them he would look into everything as needed. He even shook hands as he thanked everyone for coming. He made mental notes, like files on an already overflowing desk, because the town deserved follow through, even if he felt like he was running on fumes most days.

By the time the final resident drifted out of the chamber, the room had settled into a quiet hush. Only the custodial staff remained, moving quietly along the aisles emptying trash and straightening chairs under the soft hum of the lights.

He finally let his shoulders slump.

The room fell quiet in that way public spaces do once the people leave—still holding their warmth, no longer holding their voices. The council seal on the far wall, a lighthouse framed by waves and oak leaves, caught the overhead light. *Eden's Harbour: A City That Remembers.* The words curved around the emblem in gold leaf.

He snorted softly under his breath. His past experience reminding him that, remembering wasn't always the blessing people made it out to be.

The double doors at the back of the chamber burst open, and the familiar sound tugged him out of his thoughts. He didn't have to look to know who it was. Only one person opened those doors like the room belonged to her as much as it did to the city.

"Now you know I told you about skipping dinner, Malcolm Gerard," her tone, warm and textured with age and just enough authority to make grown men straighten up.

He turned, his lips already pulling toward a real smile this time. "Evening, Mrs. Cole."

She made her way down the center aisle unhurriedly, her small frame moving with the kind of confidence that didn't need speed. A dark wool coat lay open over her floral dress, and a knitted scarf in autumn shades was looped around her neck. Her gray hair was tucked into a wrap, a few silver curls escaping near her ears.

"And don't 'evening, Mrs. Cole' me like you didn't say you were going to stop by my house and never showed," she said, eyes narrowing at him though the corners crinkled with affection.

"I had a meeting come up," he lied easily, which was really just another way of saying he went home and stared at the wall until it was too late to pretend he wasn't doing it.

"Mm-hmm." She stopped at the bottom of the steps leading up to the platform and planted a hand on her hip. "I watched the same meeting you presided over. It ended at seven-fifteen. You live ten minutes away from me. Don't play with me, boy."

Heat pricked the back of his neck. He was the mayor of Eden's Harbour, used to negotiating contracts and managing crises, but somehow Mrs. Cole could still make him feel like the teenager caught sneaking out of the youth choir rehearsal.

"I was tired," he said finally, knowing there was no point in weaving something more elaborate. She'd smell it on him anyway.

She studied him for a bit, her eyes softening as they traced the faint shadows under his own. "Yeah," she said quietly. "I can see that."

He cleared his throat. "What brings you down here this late? The meeting's long over. You didn't have to walk through all this mess."

"Hush. I came to see you, not your little meeting." She waved a dismissive hand toward the empty chamber, then pointed it right back at him. "And don't think I didn't notice you slipping out of the last two planning sessions for the Thanksgiving Market as soon as they adjourned. Folks wanted to talk to you."

"I talked to them." He frowned lightly. "I was there."

"You were in the room," she corrected. "That's not the same thing as being there, being present."

He opened his mouth to protest, then closed it again when he remembered the way he'd stood near the back wall, arms crossed, eyes on the agenda instead of the people. He'd spoken when he needed to, joked when it fit, nodded at all the right times. He knew how to do all of the right things to seem as if he was there in the moment.

He just didn't know how to actually live in it anymore.

"The market's going to be fine," he said, sidestepping. "We approved the vendor list tonight. Public works is on board. The committee's doing a good job."

"I know they are." She tilted her head. "That's not what I'm worried about."

"Then what are you worried about?" He leaned both hands on the wooden podium, fingers resting against the smooth surface. Funny, how something as simple as that posture felt safer than standing with his arms at his sides. "Because from where I'm standing, everything's on track."

"Everything *does* look good, on paper, maybe." She climbed the first step, then the second, until she stood just below the platform with only the railing between them. Up close, he could see the faint lines of tiredness around her eyes, but also the steady light in them—like she'd seen enough in her lifetime that very little surprised her, and absolutely nothing, intimidated her.

She reached out, tapped the side of his portfolio with her knuckles. "But you forget I've known you since before any of this." Her gaze lifted to his. "You do your job, and you do it well. I appreciate that, and so does this city. But the boy who used to come knock on my door asking if I needed help taking my trash to the curb? He at least let himself feel something."

The words landed heavier than he expected. He swallowed, something in his chest tightening. "Mrs. Cole—"

"Don't 'Mrs. Cole' me in that tone either," she cut in, but her voice gentled. "I'm not fussing. I'm... observing." She searched his face, her lips pressing together. "You go to work. You go to church. You chair your meetings. You sign your papers. You show up at every ribbon-cutting and every committee launch. And yet—"

She paused, tilted her head as if trying to see around the version of himself he'd carefully constructed.

"You're not here," she finished softly. "Not really."

He looked away, the council seal suddenly very interesting. "I'm doing what I'm supposed to do."

"I know you are." She nodded slowly. "That's the part that scares me."

He bristled just a little at that. "Why would that scare you?"

"Because duty without heart will wear you down to nothing, baby," she said simply. "And right now, all I see is a man taking care of everyone else and letting himself disappear. You need to heal baby. I know it takes time, but what you've been doing isn't healthy for you. You should let people love you. Hang out, let yourself have some fun."

The custodians' quiet movements filled the silence between them for a moment—the soft clink of a trash can lid, the rolling wheels of a cart. Somewhere in the hallway outside, someone laughed as they passed by, the sound muffled by the heavy doors.

Malcolm flexed his fingers against the podium, then let them curl back into his palms. "I don't have the luxury of hanging out," he said eventually. "This city needs its mayor, especially around the holidays."

"This city needs its people," she corrected. "You just happen to be both."

He almost smiled at that. Almost.

She stepped up the last few inches so she stood even with him, close enough to touch. "Thanksgiving is coming," she said. "And those markets you just approved? The dinners? The little charity programs? All that is more than logistics and budgets and speeches. It's people loving on people. It's families gathering. It's the lonely finding a seat at the table."

Her eyes didn't leave his. "You plan to be part of that this year, or just... attend it?"

The question hit something deeper than he was ready to unpack in a half-lit council chamber.

He thought of his family's group text thread blinking on his phone, unread messages stacking up in a conversation with his sister and mother. Thought of the church announcements that went out each week, his name listed as a guest speaker for the Thanksgiving service, the congregation expecting their mayor to say something hopeful.

He thought of the empty side of his bed, the quiet at his table. The way holidays had felt like wounds instead of celebrations for the last two years.

"I'll be where I need to be," he said finally, keeping his tone even. It was the safest answer he could give without lying or telling too much of the truth.

Mrs. Cole's gaze held his, and for a moment he wondered if she could hear everything he wasn't saying.

"I know you will," she replied. "But I'm asking you to be there… here." She pressed her fingertips lightly against his chest, over the fabric of his navy suit. "Not just in your schedule."

The touch was gentle, but he still felt the urge to shift away. He didn't. Not this time.

"I don't know how to do that," he admitted quietly, surprising himself with the honesty of it.

"There it is," she murmured, more to herself than to him. "You start by telling the truth. To God. To yourself." She let her hand drop. "And maybe by not ducking out of every room the minute the formalities are over."

"I didn't duck out tonight," he said, a little defensive.

Her eyebrow shot up. "I came down here, and you were up on this stage by yourself, about to sneak out the side door. That's what we used to call 'slipping away' when I was growing up."

He huffed, the closest thing to a laugh he'd allowed himself in the last hour. "You really came just to fuss at me?"

"If I was fussing, you'd know it." Her lips twitched. "I came to make sure you saw my invitation with your own two eyes."

"What invitation?"

She pulled a folded piece of paper from her coat pocket and held it out. He took it, smoothing the creases with his thumbs. At the top, written in her looping script, were the words: **Cole Family & Friends Thanksgiving Dinner**. Beneath it, the details—time, place, a note that said *Bring nothing but yourself. I mean it.* Underlined twice.

He stared at the words a little longer than necessary. "Mrs. Cole..."

"I invite you every year," she said lightly. "You never come."

"I have a lot of obligations that day."

"I know. Church service, community dinner, photo ops." She nodded. "I'm not saying skip all that. I'm saying, when the crowds thin and the cameras are gone, you still need somewhere to sit down and be a person, not a position."

He tried to imagine walking into her house on Thanksgiving evening, being wrapped in the noise and warmth of her children and grandchildren and neighbors. Tried to picture sitting at a table that wasn't his, surrounded by people who remembered his wife and knew this would be another year she wouldn't be there.

The thought made his chest ache.

"I'll... see what I can do," he said, aware of how hollow it sounded even as it left his mouth.

Mrs. Cole narrowed her eyes again, but this time there was more sadness than annoyance in them. "You do that." She turned away, then glanced back over her shoulder. "Malcolm?"

"Ma'am?"

She held his gaze, her voice soft but edged with something that felt a lot like prayer. "I just want to see you be *you* again."she said.

He didn't have an answer for that.

She gave him one last look, called out over her shoulder, "And call your mama boy," then headed back up the aisle, pausing to exchange a few words with the custodial staff, making them laugh before she disappeared through the doors into the hallway.

The room felt quieter after she left.

Malcolm looked down at the invitation in his hand, the ink dark against the cream paper. He traced the underlined words—*Bring nothing but yourself*—and exhaled.

"Yeah," he muttered under his breath, folding the paper carefully and slipping it into his portfolio. "We'll see."

He clicked off the lights on the way out, the council chamber falling into shadows behind him as he stepped into the corridor, tie still perfectly knotted, smile back in place.

CHAPTER 2

The scent of fresh bread and roasted coffee drifted through the open doors of *Tianna's Bistro* as Malcolm stepped inside the next morning. The bell above the entrance chimed, its gentle ring instantly familiar. The bisro was one of the few places in town he could walk into without being swallowed by expectation. People still greeted him, of course—he was the mayor—but the rhythm here was slower, softer. Less formal. More human.

"Morning, Mayor." called Rebekah from behind the counter, her boho braids wrapped in a patterned scarf, a smile warm enough to cut through the late autumn chill. "The usual?"

"Yes, ma'am," he replied, taking his place in line. "Please."

She winked. "Already knew."

He didn't doubt it. Half the businesses in Eden's Harbour could probably set their clocks by him—his routines were that predictable now. Same breakfast. Same route to work. Same weekly stops.Everything controlled.

A few other patrons offered waves or nods, and he returned each one with the same polished warmth he'd given a thousand times before. Surface-level.

He took his spot the same way he always had—second table from the window--clear view of the square outside. The bistro's windows were fogged slightly from the cold, but through the glass he could see the early stirrings of the Thanksgiving Market. Volunteers carrying crates. Vendors marking their booth spots. Kids darting around, chasing each other between lampposts wrapped in garland.

A couple walked past the window, sharing a pastry, laughing at something small and sweet.

Malcolm's chest tightened before he even had time to resent it.

Rebekah brought his cup of coffee and placed his breakfast sandwich on the wooden table. "You okay today?" she asked, eyes briefly searching his face in a way that was almost too perceptive.

He gave her that easy smile, the one he'd perfected so thoroughly it rarely cracked. "Doing well. Thank you."

"You look tired," she said—not nosy, just observant. Rebekah had a way of seeing things without prying them open. "But you always look tired lately."

He offered a thin smile. "Part of the job."

"Maybe that should change," she added softly. Then she moved on, greeting the next customer in line.

When she walked away, he wrapped his hands around the warm mug, letting the heat seep into his palms. Outside, a gust of wind rustled through fallen leaves, sending a swirl of yellows and browns skating across the stone walkway.

His phone buzzed once on the table.

Mom: *Don't forget. Sunday dinner. Your nieces practiced their dance last night. They want to show Uncle Malcolm before anyone else.*

He stared at the message, jaw working as his thumb hovered over the screen.

He wasn't avoiding his family. Not exactly.

He just didn't know how to exist inside their joy anymore.

He locked the screen without responding.

Another buzz came immediately.

Mom: *No pressure. Just think about it.*

Malcolm tipped his head back, eyes closing for a breath that felt heavier than he wanted it to. He loved his mother. Loved his family.

But being around all that love made the quiet corners of his life feel sharper.

He opened his eyes and returned his attention to the square outside.

A group of teenagers pushed through the bistro door, the wind carrying their laughter with them. They were loud in the way teenagers could be, fresh from school and free for the afternoon. One girl—maybe sixteen—called out:

"Hey, Mayor Mouton!"

He raised a hand in greeting. "Afternoon."

"You coming to the community dinner this year?" she asked, grabbing a muffin from the pastry case. "They said you might give the opening welcome again."

"We'll see," he replied.

"Hope you do! You make it feel official." She grinned and headed to her seat.

He wasn't sure if that made him feel appreciated... or boxed in.

He glanced out the window again. A volunteer tripped over a bundled extension cord and laughed it off, two others helping her steady herself.

Family.

Connection.

Belonging.

It used to be the kind of moment his wife would notice first, pressing her cold hands to his cheeks when he pretended not to smile and whispering, "See? This town loves its people."

His chest tightened.

A soft thump landed in front of him as Rebekah set down a warm pastry wrapped in parchment.

"I didn't order this," he said.

"Nope. But you look like you need it." She leaned her hip against the table. "And before you make some polite speech about not wanting to take free things, it's the one I burned slightly at the edge. I wasn't gonna sell it anyway."

He huffed. "How generous of you."

She smiled. "Look, I'm not gonna pry, Malcolm. But... if you ever want to sit in the back and not be 'the mayor' for a minute, you're welcome to."

His brows lowered. "Would that even be possible?"

"It would when I kick everyone else out, just say the word" she teased.

He chuckled—not forced this time. "I appreciate it."

"Good." She squeezed his shoulder lightly and moved on.

He took a bite of the pastry. Cinnamon and brown sugar. Comfort he didn't ask for but strangely needed.

Outside, the vendors were almost done setting up their morning staging. A little boy carried a cardboard turkey almost as tall as he was, wobbling as he crossed the square. Another child ran behind him, shouting encouragement.

Malcolm found himself staring a bit longer than he intended.

Children didn't hide emotions. Families didn't pretend not to care. This town didn't pretend not to care.

Maybe he'd forgotten how to stand in the middle of that without breaking apart.

His phone buzzed again, but he didn't look at it.

Instead, he picked up his coffee, and—for the first time in weeks—he allowed himself to simply sit in the moment. No agenda. No schedule. No speeches.

Just Malcolm.

Just a man trying to remember what it felt like toenjoy life

Chapter 3

The community center's main hall was already half-full when Malcolm arrived that afternoon. Long tables had been arranged into rows, covered with clipboards, donation forms, and paper cups of cooling coffee. Voices blended into a warm hum—volunteers discussing booth layouts, teenagers arguing good-naturedly about poster designs, members of the planning committee flipping through binders with practiced efficiency.

Eden's Harbour in its most natural habitat: preparing for the Holidays together.

Malcolm paused just inside the doorway, letting the scene wash over him. It wasn't the crowd that gave him pause—it was the ease. The effortless way people moved around each other, checking in, laughing, belonging.

Then someone noticed him.

"Mayor Mouton! Good to see you."Mr. Lawrence, the planning chair, waved him over with the enthusiasm of a man who'd had too much coffee and too little sleep.

Malcolm nodded politely and walked toward the front. "Afternoon, everyone."

A few scattered "hi, Mayors" and "good afternoons" floated back at him. People smiled in that warm but respectful way the town always did around him—not stiff, just aware.

"Thanks for stopping in," Lawrence said, adjusting his glasses as he glanced at the agenda. "We're just going over vendor placements for the Thanksgiving Market. Public Works sent over updated diagrams if you want a look."

"Let's see them," Malcolm replied.

Lawrence handed him a marked-up map of the square, sections labeled in bright marker. Malcolm studied it, tapping a finger lightly against his chin. "You might want to shift the children's craft area closer to the fountain," he said. "Better light in the afternoon, and it won't block the vendor traffic here."

Lawrence's eyebrows lifted. "Good call. I'll make a note."

A few volunteers glanced over, murmuring approval. It was small, but Malcolm felt something like... contribution. Not showmanship. Not public-facing responsibility. Just genuine input.

A cluster of teens at the side table laughed loudly over construction paper turkeys. One of them—a girl with long braids—looked up and waved. "Hey, Mayor!"

He lifted a hand in return. "Hey there."

"You coming to help us paint the mural next week?" she asked with hopeful eyes.

He hesitated. For once, he didn't use his usual line of *We'll see*.

"I might," he said instead.

She grinned like he'd just promised her the moon.

Lawrence shifted his binder and cleared his throat. "Next on the agenda is the volunteer rotation schedule. We need extra hands for—"

The doors opened behind them, letting in a gust of cold air and a group of college students. They brought noise with them—good noise—arms full of donation boxes, cheeks flushed from the walk.

One of them, a young woman with thick curls and a knitted beanie, stopped short when she saw Malcolm. Her eyes widened a little.

"Mayor Mouton?" she said, stepping forward.

He gave a polite smile. "Afternoon."

"I didn't think I'd see you here," she said, shifting her box to her other hip. "I'm glad you came."

He nodded once. "It's good to be here."

She hesitated, then added softly, "I knew your wife."

The words hit him like a sound only he could hear—quiet, sharp, slicing through the comfortable background murmur.

For a moment he was back in her classroom, listening to her talk about stories and letting her students feel seen. She always said teaching wasn't a job for her; it was more like her ministry.

He stood still.

The young woman's eyes softened. "She was my high school English teacher. Mrs. Mouton. She... she helped me a lot during my junior year."

Malcolm wet his lips, forcing them not to tremble. "Did she?"

"Yes." A small smile tugged at her mouth. "She always said stories were how people learned to feel safe telling the truth, and a good writer creates a story they love first. I never forgot that."

He swallowed, the motion thick.

"I thought you'd want to know," she added gently. "She made a difference."

A heavy silence settled between them. A quiet honoring.

"Thank you," Malcolm said finally, his voice lower than he intended.

"Of course." She stepped back, giving him space, before joining her group at the table.

Malcolm exhaled slowly, grounding himself with a hand braced against the back of a chair. The room hadn't changed. No one else had noticed the exchange. But something inside him had shifted—just a fraction, just enough to sting.

Lawrence cleared his throat. "Mayor? You alright?"

Malcolm straightened, smoothing his expression. "Yes. I'm fine."

They returned to discussing rotation schedules, donation drop-off locations, and booth setup procedures. Malcolm nodded at appropriate moments, offered insights when needed, and listened as volunteers shared updates.

But part of him remained lodged in that one brief memory someone else had carried all these years.

His wife. Her classroom. The way she loved people through gentle guidance and encouragement. The way she saw people.

The way he'd been avoiding being seen since she died.

When the meeting wrapped, volunteers packed their things, still chattering. Malcolm walked out with them, the chatter fading as he stepped into the cold late-afternoon light. The wind tugged at his coat collar, the sky heavy with the promise of early evening.

He didn't go straight to his car.

Instead, he stopped at the edge of the square, watching the vendors across the street rearrange bins and straighten tablecloths.

Families moved together with effortless connection.Children ran through piles of leaves someone had raked earlier.Teens decorated a cardboard booth with paint-splattered fingers.A couple carried a crate between them, laughing the whole way.

Malcolm stood perfectly still, the weight in his chest both familiar and newly stirred.

He wasn't jealous of their joy.

He just missed his own.

And that... he finally let himself acknowledge.

Chapter 4

The prayer garden behind the historic church wasn't large, but it didn't need to be. A stone path curved between tall shrubs and late-autumn flowers, most of them already closing for the season. Wind chimes hung from a nearby magnolia tree, the soft tinkling drifting through the air like a fragile melody.

Malcolm stood at the entrance for a moment, hands in his coat pockets, breath clouding the cold air.

He hadn't meant to come here. He'd only been driving home from the community center when something made him turn into the church lot. Maybe it was the heaviness in his chest. Maybe it was the way the student's words had dug under his armor. Maybe it was God nudging him in a way he wasn't ready to say out loud.

Either way, he was here, at one of *her* favorite places to be.

He walked the path slowly, the crunch of loose gravel beneath his shoes grounding him. Every bench he passed seemed to invite him to sit, to stop pretending, to stop performing.

The last time he walked this path in late November, she'd slipped her hand into his and teased him about how the garden smelled different the week of Thanksgiving—"like cold hope," she said, laughing when he rolled his eyes.

He hadn't understood it then, but he did now.

Passing up the first two benches, he finally took a seat at the third.

The air smelled faintly of cedar. Somewhere beyond the trees, a choir was rehearsing in the sanctuary — voices rising and falling in harmonies that seemed to warm him in the cold night air.

Malcolm rested his elbows on his knees and rubbed his hands together, letting the warmth build between his palms.

It had been a long time since he'd allowed himself to sit and just breathe.

A very long time.

He exhaled, the sound rougher than he intended. "Lord...I know I haven't talked with you in a long time... I don't even know where to start."

The wind chimes answered for him.

"I'm tired," he whispered. "feel like I'm living off of fumes, whatever is less than empty, that's what I feel right now."

His throat tightened. He blinked slowly, eyes lowering to the ground at his feet.

"I do everything I'm supposed to. I show up. I work. I smile. I serve. I'm there for everyone. But internally..." He swallowed. "... I'm miles away."

A leaf flew across the path and landed near his shoe.

His voice dropped even lower. "And I know people mean well. I know they care. But when they look at me... they see the part of my life that's gone. And I don't... I don't know how to deal with that."

He closed his eyes.

Her face resurfaced first, then her laugh.

Then her voice.Her classroom.Her handwriting in the margins of old books.Her gentle hum when she cooked.The way she'd rest her head on his chest while they were watching a movie together.

The last Thanksgiving they'd shared — the house full of family, full of life.

His breath hitched, barely audible.

"I miss her," he said softly, the words cracking at the edges. "I miss her every minute. And being around families... being around love like that..." He paused, chest tightening. "It makes me feel like I'm watching the world through a door I can't walk through."

The breeze picked up, sweeping a scatter of leaves down the path.

Tears welled up in his eyes, but he didn't fall apart. That wasn't how Malcolm broke.He broke quietly — in the tightening of his jaw, the way he steadied his breath, the way he pressed his fingers together like someone trying to hold themselves in place.

"I don't want pity," he said. "I don't want people looking at me like I'm fragile. I just—" His eyes lifted to the sky. "I just want to feel... something again. I want, no I *need* this feeling of emptiness to go."

He wiped the tears from his eyes as the silence settled around him.

The choir's voices drifted through the trees — a hymn he hadn't heard in a long time.

Strength for today, and bright hope for tomorrow...

He leaned back against the bench, eyes closing as the words washed over him.

After a moment, he released a long breath. "Help me find my way back. That's all I'm asking."

It wasn't eloquent or polished. It wasn't the kind of prayer a mayor might give at a podium. It was honest, raw and real.

It was the first prayer he'd prayed from the heart in years.

When he finally stood, the weight in his chest hadn't disappeared, but it felt a little less heavy.

It felt like hope.Something like the first spark of light coming back into his life.

Malcolm brushed off his coat and walked the path back toward his car. The wind was colder now, the sky dimming into early evening.

But for the first time in a long time, he didn't feel so somber.

Chapter 5

The following week moved quickly in Eden's Harbour, the kind of pre-holiday hustle that made the town feel alive from sunup to sundown. Leaves swirled across the sidewalks in golden drifts, carrying the promise of winter, and the tall oak trees downtown had been wrapped in strands of soft white lights that flickered against the early evening sky.

Malcolm hadn't planned to show up early to the Thanksgiving Market prep day.

But he did.

He wasn't sure why, whether it was habit, obligation, or maybe something deeper. The prayer garden hadn't solved anything overnight, but it had loosened something inside him. Enough that showing up didn't feel quite so heavy or obligatory.

The square was already bustling when he arrived. Cars unloading boxes. Kids weaving between folding tables. Volunteers tugging at tent stakes and smoothing out tablecloths. An organized kind of chaos.

"Morning, Mayor," called Mr. Jefferson, a retired machinist tightening a banner overhead.

"Morning," Malcolm replied, offering a small wave as he stepped onto the cobblestone walkway.

He didn't hover at the edges today. He walked straight into the middle of the activity, hands in his coat pockets, watching the setup unfold like a moving tapestry.

"Hey, Mayor! Can you hold this for a second?" a teenage boy shouted, juggling a roll of string lights and a ladder far too tall for him.

Malcolm caught the ladder just in time. "You sure about this?" he asked.

"Nope. That's why I'm asking for help," the boy laughed.

It was impossible not to huff a quiet laugh in return. "Fair enough."

He braced the ladder as the teen climbed and started securing lights along the wooden archway that would mark the entrance to the Market. A group of younger kids cheered every time a new strand lit up, even if it flickered.

"Perfect!" the boy said, climbing down. "Thanks, Mayor."

"Anytime."

He meant it.

He wasn't used to meaning it.

Across the square, someone shouted in playful frustration. Malcolm turned to see Rebekah wrestling a box of pie tins while her daughter—Tianna, quick-footed and dramatic—tried her best to supervise.

"No, Mama, that stack goes on *this* table!" Tianna said, hands flying.

"They're the same table," Rebekah countered, pushing one curl away from her eyes with the back of her wrist. "Same height, same shape—"

"But *this one* feels better," Tianna insisted.

Malcolm couldn't help the small smile tugging at his mouth. He walked over. "Need a hand?"

Rebekah shook a loose braid from her face and laughed. "I will take every hand that's offered."

He lifted the heavy box with ease, setting it on the correct table—according to Tianna.

"Thank you!" Tianna said, snapping her fingers dramatically as if assigning him gold stars. "Mayor Mouton, you have excellent table instincts."

"Oh, now *he* has instincts, and what do I have?" Rebekah teased.

Tianna rolled her eyes and skipped away to join a group of girls painting wooden signs.

Rebekah adjusted one of the tins and glanced up at him. "You doing okay today?"

"Yeah," he said, surprised to realize it wasn't entirely a lie. "Actually... yeah, I think so."

"Good." She nudged him with her elbow. "You deserve a good day."

He didn't know what to do with that. So he nodded and focused on the tables.

Volunteers moved around him, shifting stacks of supplies, unpacking decorations, humming to the background music playing from a portable speaker. Somewhere behind him, a choir group rehearsed a few lines of their Thanksgiving opener—warm harmonies floating through the air.

The sounds of the town. The heart of it.

And for once, he didn't feel like he was standing outside of it.

A voice broke through his thoughts.

"Mayor! We need one more set of hands over here!"

He turned and saw the college students from the planning meeting—boxes in hand, smiles bright and familiar. The young woman who had recognized his wife waved him over.

He hesitated only a second... and then walked toward them.

They handed him a crate of canned goods for the donation station. As he set it down, the young woman gave him a small, warm smile.

"You doing alright?" she asked quietly.

He nodded once. "I'm getting there."

"That's good," she said, and turned back to her group.

Simple. Gentle. No digging into his wounds.

He appreciated that more than she knew.

As the sun climbed higher, the Market began to take shape. Tables stood decorated, lights hung, volunteers buzzed around completing their tasks. Malcolm found himself moving from station to station, not because anyone expected it of him, but because he wanted to help.

Halfway through tying a garland, Mr. Lawrence approached with a clipboard.

"Mayor, wanted to say... it's good to see you today."

"Appreciate that," Malcolm said.

Lawrence nodded, lingering for a thoughtful moment. "You know, you don't always have to carry everything alone. Most of the people in this town care for you and wouldn't mind helping you."

Malcolm didn't know what to say to that.

So he gave a small nod.

Lawrence patted his shoulder and walked away.

The weight pressed into Malcolm's chest again—but this time it didn't crush him. It settled differently. Less like grief, more like being seen.

He closed the last loop of garland around a post and stepped back. The square looked beautiful.

And being part of it...didn't feel like pretending.

It felt natural, like a part of him was coming back.

CHAPTER 6

The morning settled over the town with a thin veil of silver clouds stretching across the sky. By late afternoon, the square had emptied of volunteers, leaving behind the soft glow of lights and the quiet hum of a town ready for tomorrow.

Malcolm stood at the edge of the cobblestone walkway, hands buried deep in his coat pockets as he took in the scene. The tents were neatly aligned, banners fluttered gently, and the scent of cinnamon drifted faintly in the cold air. Someone had left the fountain lights on, casting ripples of gold across the surface of the water.

It felt peaceful. A few lingering volunteers walked by carrying empty boxes. They waved and he waved back.

"Happy Thanksgiving, Mayor!"

"You too," he replied, offering a nod as they disappeared down the street.

He walked toward the fountain, drawn to its soft glow. The closer he got, the more he felt the weight in his chest shift — not heavier, not lighter, just... shifting. He lowered himself onto the stone ledge, elbows on his knees, letting the cool mist brush against his face.

Families passed by in small clusters, heading home with cakes and pies carefully balanced in their hands. Children ran ahead of their parents, scarves flying, laughter spilling into the quiet streets. Couples walked arm in arm, whispering about plans for tomorrow.

And Malcolm sat still, watching life move around him.

A boy — maybe seven or eight — wandered near the fountain, holding a small paper turkey colored wildly outside the lines. He paused when he saw Malcolm, eyes widening a little.

"You're the mayor," the boy said.

Malcolm smiled faintly. "That's what they tell me."

The boy stepped closer and held out the turkey. "We made these in school. My teacher said to give one to somebody who helps people."

Malcolm blinked, surprised. "You're sure you want to give it to me?"

The boy nodded enthusiastically. "You help everybody. That's what my mom says."

Warmth spread through Malcolm's chest, subtle and unexpected. He accepted the paper turkey carefully.

"Thank you," he said, voice gentler than before. "I'm honored."

The boy grinned and rushed back to join his family, leaving Malcolm alone again with the fountain's light and the soft rustle of garland overhead.

He looked down at the paper turkey — uneven, messy, full of effort and innocence. A simple gesture. A small reminder that people saw him. Not the title. Not the mask. *Him.*

Warmth spread through Malcolm's chest, subtle and unexpected—stirring the same quiet place his wife used to reach whenever her students brought home crooked drawings and misspelled notes. Their fridge had once been covered in them, a gallery of small hands and big hearts.

This little turkey felt like one more piece of what he thought he'd lost...and what he might be finding again.

His phone buzzed.

> **Mom:** *Dinner is at 3 Sunday if you change your mind. The girls practiced their dance some more. They want to show you.*

He stared at the message for a moment, thumb hovering over the screen before he set the phone beside him on the ledge.

He wasn't ready to respond.But he wasn't shrinking from the invitation anymore either.

The breeze shifted, brushing past him, ruffling the corners of the little paper turkey in his hands. He leaned back slightly, eyes lifting to the sky. A single star had slipped through the clouds, faint but present.

The kind of star you only noticed when you stopped long enough to look.

He inhaled slowly, letting the cold air steady him.

Tomorrow would come whether he was ready or not.Bu t maybe, just maybe, he could meet it as himself and not the version he thought he had to be.

As he stood, the paper turkey carefully tucked into his coat pocket, he took one last look at the square glowing quietly under the early evening sky.

It felt like a place he belonged to, and a place that still had room for him, even in the quiet spaces.

He turned and walked toward his car, the sound of distant laughter trailing after him like a soft reminder:

He wasn't as alone as he thought.

Chapter 7

The day of the town's Thanksgiving Market arrived with a crisp, golden light breaking through the thin veil of clouds that hung over Eden's Harbour. The town was already awake by the time Malcolm stepped outside—flashes of orange and red leaves swirling through the streets, early risers carrying pies and trays from their cars into the community center, families bundled in scarves heading toward the square.

He locked his door, hesitated only a moment, then pocketed his keys.

This was the first Thanksgiving in a long time where he wasn't bracing himself for the day. He wasn't excited, but he also wasn't dreading it. He was more so... open. Open to whatever the day wold bring.

And that was something.

As he walked through downtown, the familiar sights and sounds wrapped around him—sweet potato pies cooling on bakery racks, children holding painted turkey masks, the church bells chiming lightly in the distance.

By the time he reached the square, the Thanksgiving Market was in full bloom. Music floated through the crisp air, families carried dishes in foil trays, and laughter rippled between each tent like threads stitching the town together.

Children in knitted hats raced each other across the cobblestones, nearly colliding with a volunteer setting out cups and cider. A group of teens decorated a wooden sign with last-minute paint strokes, making the turkey on it look more eccentric than festive. And across the way, the church choir rehearsed warm-up harmonies for the afternoon program.

The whole scene vibrated with life.

"Morning, Mayor!" someone called from behind a table stacked with sweet potato pies.

"Morning," he replied, waving.

Several others greeted him as he made his way toward the central tent. No one hovered. No one stared too long. No one treated him like a fragile ornament. They treated him like... part of the town.

A hand tapped his shoulder lightly. "Mayor Mouton?"

He turned to see Mr. Lawrence holding a clipboard, his breath forming small clouds in the cold air.

"We're ready for the welcome whenever you are," Lawrence said. "No rush, we just want to give families time to settle."

Malcolm exhaled quietly and nodded. "Alright. Let's do it."

Lawrence stepped away to adjust the microphone stand. Malcolm approached the platform slowly, giving himself a moment to steady his breath. The crowd was gathering, not a massive group, but enough families and neighbors to fill the square with warmth.

When he stepped up, the soft chatter quieted. Faces lifted. Smiles formed.

The town wasn't waiting for perfection. Just presence.

He cleared his throat gently. "Good morning, Eden's Harbour. Happy Thanksgiving."

A wave of murmured greetings rolled back to him.

He rested his hands on the podium.

"I'll be brief," he began. "I know the food smells too good to keep you long."

A few chuckles rose from the crowd.

"This year... well, it's been a lot for many of us. Some have lost, some have changed, and some of us are still learning how to live with both."

He paused, letting his words breathe.

"But what I love about this town is the way we show up for each other. Not just on the good days, but on the bad ones too."

Heads nodded. Warmly and softly.

"I'm grateful," he continued, voice steady. "For this community. For the love you give so freely. For the way you look out for your neighbors. And for the way you remind us all that we don't walk this journey alone."

His throat tightened slightly, but he didn't run from it.

"Today, I hope you find something to be thankful for... even if it's small. Sometimes the smallest things carry the most love."

He bowed his head. "Let's pray."

He led a short, humble prayer — not rehearsed, not formal. Just an honest, from his heart, prayer.

When he finished, a soft "Amen" rose from the crowd like a warm tide.

As people moved toward the long tables, filling plates and exchanging greetings, Malcolm stepped down from the platform and slipped into the flow of movement. A little girl tugged at the sleeve of his coat as he passed.

"Mr. Mayor, will you sit with us?" she asked, pointing to her family's table decorated with paper place-mats and crayon drawings of turkeys.

He smiled gently. "I will."

He followed her, taking a seat at the edge of the long table. Children laughed. Parents talked. Someone cracked a joke about losing count of how many pies were on the dessert table. A group of teens passed around a pitcher of iced tea like a prized treasure.

Malcolm took a quiet breath and let himself settle into the moment.

He didn't feel out of place or overexposed.He didn't feel like a mayor pressed into performance.

He just felt... present.

A neighbor handed him a plate already filled with food. "You've done a good job this year," she said softly. "We're all grateful for you."

He nodded, the words warming him more than the food ever could.

He continued to eat, observing the laughter around him. He paid close attention to the families as they passed their plates around and realized moments like these were what made space for hope to come back into his life.

He could hear his wife's words eching in his thoughts, *"community was God's way of reminding people they weren't meant to walk this life alone."* He hadn't understood the truth of that until this moment, standing in a room full of warmth and love that he'd spend two year sidestepping.

For the first time since losing her, his gratitude didn't feel forced.

CHAPTER 8

The sun had already dipped below the rooftops by the time Malcolm walked through his front door. The warmth of the Thanksgiving Market still clung to him—faint echoes of laughter, the murmur of conversation, the soft tug of children pulling him toward craft tables.

The house greeted him with its usual quiet.

But tonight... it didn't feel as heavy.

He set his keys in the bowl by the door and shrugged off his coat, and hung it neatly in the coat closet. A candle he'd lit that morning still faintly scented the air with cedar and vanilla. The soft glow from the lamp in the living room spread across the wood floors like a gentle invitation.

He hadn't planned on staying long at the Market. He certainly hadn't expected to enjoy himself. But somehow, surrounded by the town's warmth, he had felt something shift—small, quiet, steady.

He moved to the couch and sank into the cushions, letting his body exhale fully for the first time all day. He rested his hands on his knees, staring at nothing in particular, the silence filling in around him like a soft blanket.

After a long moment, he walked back to the closet, reached into his coat pocket and pulled out the little paper turkey the boy had given him earlier. The crayon colors were uneven, the edges bent from being handled with small, eager fingers.

He smoothed the corner gently.

Somebody who helps people.

The words echoed in his mind.

He rubbed a hand over his jaw, emotions rising and pulling back like a tide. For so long, he'd felt disconnected from everything—responsibility without purpose, service without sincerity. But today... today felt different.

He walked to the small bookshelf by the window, and opened the lower cabinet. A stack of journals and letters rested inside, untouched for months—maybe longer.

He hesitated before taking out one journal, the leather worn, the edges soft from years of use. His wife's handwriting marked the cover in small looping script.

He sat back on the couch, the journal heavy in his hands.

He opened it slowly, the familiar scent of old paper drifting up. Inside were bits of her world—classroom notes, scriptures written in the margins, reminders she'd left for herself, small doodles of flowers when she was thinking.

Halfway through, a sticky note slipped free and fluttered onto his lap.

Her handwriting swept across the square page:

"One day at a time, Malcolm.Grace is patient."

She had loved Thanksgiving. Not for the food, but because it was the one day she could convince him to slow down long enough to enjow what they had built. *"Traditions keeps the magic alive,"* she'd tell him, nudging his shoulder whenever her tried to rush through the day.

His breath stilled.

His eyes stung—not with sharp pain, but with something softer. Something like release.

He traced the words with his thumb.

"I'm trying," he whispered into the quiet. "I really am."

The room held the moment gently, like it understood.

His phone buzzed on the coffee table.

Mom:*We hope you had a good day, baby. We love you. Don't forget about dinner Sunday, if you want to stop by. No pressure. Just come as you are.*

He stared at the message.

He let the journal rest beside him as he typed:

Malcolm: *I'd like that. See you then.*

The response came almost immediately.

Mom: *Good. We've missed you. Love you.*

He leaned back against the cushions, letting the words wash over him.

He hadn't been ready before.Maybe he wasn't fully ready now. But he was willing.

And sometimes, willingness was enough for grace to stand on.

He turned off the lamp, leaving only the soft glow of the candle flickering across the room. As he made his way to the bedroom, the house didn't feel quite so empty.

Not because anything had changed on the outside, but because something had finally shifted inside him, and he was beginning to let people back in.

Chapter 9

The smell of cornbread and baked chicken reached Malcolm before he even stepped onto his mother's porch. Warm light spilled through the front windows, and the low hum of conversation floated into the cool evening air. He paused at the bottom step, one hand gripping the railing.

It had been months since he'd been here on a Sunday.

Too long.

He exhaled slowly, then climbed the steps and knocked lightly, though he knew he didn't have to.

The door swung open before his knuckles touched it again.

"There he is!" His mother's voice filled the doorway, soft but full, layered with a joy he hadn't realized he'd missed. "Get on in here, baby."

She didn't pull him into one of her tight embraces—not yet. She rested her hand on his arm first, as if checking the temperature of the moment, making sure he was ready.

He was. Maybe for the first time.

The living room was alive with warmth—his sister on the couch scrolling through her phone; his brother at the dining table laughing at something on TV; his nieces darting across the room in socks that slid too easily on the hardwood floors.

"Uncle Malcolm!"

Two small bodies collided with his legs. He steadied himself, surprised by the force of their excitement.

"We learned a dance!" the younger one announced. "Wanna see? Mama said we could show you first!"

He crouched down slightly and smiled. "I'd love to."

They scrambled back toward the kitchen, giggling. His sister looked over from the couch, eyebrows raised in mock shock.

"Look who decided to join the land of the living," she teased.

He shook his head, chuckling. "Good to see you too, Nessa."

She stood and hugged him—quick and warm.

In the kitchen, his mother moved from pot to oven with ease. "Fix you a plate, baby," she said, pointing with a wooden spoon. "The food's still hot."

He took a plate from the stack on the counter. "Smells amazing."

"When does it not?" she said with a small smile.

He stood at the kitchen counter longer than neccedary, staring at the empty plate he'd set out without thinking. Michelle used to fuss at him for never plating anything neatly on holidays. *Malcolm, it's Thanksgiving, not as bachelor potluck,"* she'd tease, taking over before he could argue.

The memory drifted in, warming the stillness around him.

He filled his plate; cornbread, mac and cheese, baked chicken, green beans cooked with smoked turkey. They all gathered around the table a few minutes later. His nieces insisted on performing their dance before anyone touched a fork. It was chaotic, full of missed steps and exaggerated spins, but the girls beamed the entire time.

Malcolm clapped along with everyone else, genuine warmth spreading through him.

His mother watched him from the head of the table, eyes soft and full of love.

"You want to say grace?" she asked quietly, careful with the offering.

For a moment, he thought about declining. Out of habit. Out of fear of being too exposed.

But he nodded. "Yeah. I can."

Everyone bowed their heads.

His voice was steady. "Lord, thank You for this food. Thank You for family. Thank You for... another chance to be present. Bless this home. Bless everyone here. Amen."

"Amen," they echoed.

Dinner was easy and filled with laughter and storytelling and second helpings.His brother teased him about being a celebrity at the Thanksgiving Market.His sister threatened to run for mayor just to "see if she could do it better."His mother kept touching his shoulder as she passed by, the small gestures of a woman grateful to have her child at her table again.

At the end of the meal, as plates were stacked and leftovers were packed into containers, his mom pulled him aside near the sink.

"I'm glad you came," she said softly.

"Me too."

She touched his cheek gently, her thumb brushing the edge of his beard. "You don't have to be so strong all the time, Malcolm. Not here."

"I know Mama," he said. And for once, he meant it.

She smiled and hugged him—tight, like she'd been saving that embrace for months.

When he left later that night, stepping out into the cold air with a container of leftovers and a full heart, he realized something:

thing:

He didn't feel like he was watching life from the outside any-more. He felt as if he was slowly becoming a part of it again.

Chapter 10

The next afternoon, Malcolm found himself driving without a destination in mind. The sky was a cool, pale gray, the kind that hinted at winter without fully committing. The roads were quiet, most families still lingering over their second wave of leftovers or lounging inside with holiday movies and blankets.

He wasn't sure where he was going until he got there.

The cemetery sat on a gentle hill just outside Eden's Harbour, the iron gate still decorated with autumn garland from earlier in the season. He parked beside an old oak tree and stepped out of the car, the cold air brushing across his face like a familiar whisper.

He took slow steps along the gravel path, hands in his pockets, shoulders relaxed rather than tense.

He had avoided this place for months.Not because he didn't care.But because being here felt like staring grief in the eye.

Today... he felt ready.

He found her plot easily — second row from the magnolia tree, the one that always bloomed early in spring. Her headstone was simple, elegant, carved with a small open book near the top.

Michelle Elena Mouton

Beloved Wife.Teacher.Light in many lives.

He stood for a long moment without speaking, letting the quiet settle around him. The breeze shifted, stirring the last few leaves clinging stubbornly to the magnolia's branches.

Finally, he lowered himself to sit on the cool stone bench beside the plot.

"Hey," he said softly. "It's been a while."

The air felt still, as though it was listening.

"I went to Sunday dinner yesterday." His hands rubbed together slowly. "The girls did their dance. You would've loved it."

A small smile tugged at the corner of his mouth.

"They both have your rhythm," he added. "God help them."

He exhaled, breath visible in the cold.

"I've been... trying," he said honestly. "Trying to figure out what life looks like now. Trying to be more than just the man everyone sees in public. Trying to let people in again."

He looked down at his hands.

"It hasn't been easy."A pause."But I'm getting there."

The wind chimes hanging from the magnolia tree clinked gently.

He reached into his coat pocket and pulled out the little paper turkey the child had given him. He placed it gently on the corner of her headstone, holding it steady until the wind let it settle.

"A kid gave this to me at the Market," he said with a soft laugh. "Said it was for someone who helps people. I'm not sure I deserve that yet."His voice softened. "But I'm trying to."

He leaned back slightly, eyes tracing the sky above the trees.

"I miss you," he whispered. "Not the pain of losing you... but the warmth of having you. There's a difference, I think."

It was the first time he'd said that out loud.

"And I just... wanted you to know that I am working on moving forward, on living without you. Even on the days it feels like I just may lose it."

He brushed a thumb against the edge of the bench.

"I hope that honors you."

The wind picked up for a moment, soft and cold, brushing across his shoulders like a touch.

"I just wish you were still here Chelle. I wish God had healed you on *this* side. I wasn't ready for you to go, to not be able to continue building a life with you."

He cried silently, putting his face in his palms.

He sat up, pulling a handkerchief from his coat pocket and wiped his eyes. "This was an adjustment I wasn't ready to make, but I am getting there."

After a while, he stood from the bench, brushing off the legs of his pants. He touched the top of the headstone gently.

"I'll come by again soon," he murmured. "I promise."

As he walked back toward his car, the heaviness he'd expected didn't follow him.Instead, a quiet peace settled in its place — thin, fragile, but undeniably real.

And for the first time since she'd passed, he left this place not burdened, but lighter.

As though grief had finally shifted enough to make room for something else.

Chapter 11

Thanksgiving morning broke in quiet. Malcolm had woken earlier than he expected. He sat in the living room for a long moment, watching sunlight creep across the floorboards, feeling the weight and the lightness of the week settle together in his chest.

Monday had taken something out of him. Visiting the cemetery always did. But he'd walked away with a steadiness he hadn't felt in a while—like something inside him had finally unclenched. He wasn't whole, not yet, but he wasn't suspended anymore either. Today felt... possible.

By early afternoon, he was dressed and standing at the bottom of Mrs. Cole's walkway, the small ivory invitation tucked between his fingers.

The walkway was lined with potted chrysanthemums she always brought out in the fall, burgundy and gold and deep burnt orange.

Voices drifted from inside the house—laughter, music, the distant thump of footsteps. The screen door rattled once as someone passed behind it.

He stood at the bottom of the porch longer than he meant to, breathing in the cold air.

Last year he'd avoided gatherins and anything that reminded him of walking up steps beside someone who no longer walked with him. She used to strighten his tie right before they knocked, whispering, *"Smile, Malcolm. They love you."*

Malcolm exhaled slowly, then climbed the steps and knocked.

Mrs. Cole opened the door before he could lower his hand. "Well," she said, grinning from ear to ear, "look who finally decided to stop standing in his own way."

He lifted the invitation with a crooked smile. "Am I still invited?"

She swatted the air. "Yes, even though you're late. Get in this house before all the food is gone."

He stepped inside and warmth met him like an embrace.

The house was full but not crowded, lively but not overwhelming. The smell of turkey, dressing, sweet potatoes, and something sweet and spiced drifted through the rooms. Mrs. Cole's dining table was covered in a burnt-orange runner with candles glowing low down the middle. Gospel music hummed in the background, the soft, familiar kind his grandmother used to play.

His mother spotted him first.

"Told you he'd come," she said to someone standing beside her. She wiped her hands on a dish towel and made her way over. His sister and brother looked up from the kitchen island, and the church members near the window waved when they noticed him.

And just like that, Malcolm wasn't on the outside looking in anymore.

No one hesitated. No one asked where he'd been these past few years. No one lingered on the silence he'd kept after his wife died. They just smiled at him—real, warm, simple—and shifted to make room.

Mrs. Cole pressed a plate into his hands. "Sit wherever you want, baby. And don't ask what's in the dressing. Who do you think taught your mama how to make it?" she laughed

His mother chuckled softly. "You're right about it."

I remember Chelle's dressing, it never tasted the same twice, she always called it *"spirit-led cooking."* Malcolm smiled, looking off into the distance. The familiar scent scraped at memories he hadn't planned to touch today.

"She use to add a little too much sage," his mom chuckled, pulling him out of his memory.

"Stop it Mama. I loved her dressing." he smiled

He looked at her, really looked, noticing the faint weariness in her eyes and the strength under it. "Smells like home," he said quietly.

"Good," she replied, touching his arm. "You deserve a little bit of that today."

They found their seats at the table just as the last of the dishes were placed down. His sister passed rolls to Mrs. Cole's grand-daughter. His brother cracked some joke about the Cowboys' yearly Thanksgiving heartbreak, and half the table groaned. Someone's toddler yelled, "Amen!" at the wrong time, and the whole room shook with laughter.

And Malcolm... he felt himself settling. Not shrinking into a corner, away from the crowd, but fully engaged and actually enjoying himself.

Halfway through dinner, his mother leaned closer. She didn't speak right away, just rested her hand over his. Her thumb brushed his knuckles the way she used to when he was little and bothered over something.

"I know today isn't easy," she said softly. "But I'm proud of you for being here."

He swallowed, eyes on his plate. "I'm trying, Mama."

"I know. And baby," she whispered, "trying counts. More than you think."

He looked up, meeting her gaze. There was no pity there. No pressure. Just an understanding only someone who had lived through loss could give.

"I used to think showing up would hurt more," he said.

"Sometimes it does. Sometimes it heals," she said. "Today? I think it's doing a little of both."

He exhaled through his nose, letting the truth of that land in him.

After dinner, he found himself at the edge of the living room, watching the swirl of family—his and Mrs. Cole's—intermingle like they'd been doing it for years. His sister helped Mrs. Cole slice pie. His brother was teaching one of the grandkids how to throw a soft football across the room without knocking anything over. Church members were exchanging recipes. His mother was laughing—actually laughing—with Mrs. Cole's oldest son about something Malcolm had missed entirely.

And no one treated him like he was fragile or broken or out of place. They treated him like he was theirs.

Mrs. Cole slipped beside him, folding her arms. "*This,*" she *waved around the room,* "is what happens when you stop hiding," she murmured.

"I wasn't hiding," he said, though he knew better.

She angled her head. "You weren't living either."

He didn't argue.

She nudged him with her shoulder. "Your wife loved you too much for you to stay locked in that quiet. You honor her by stepping back into the light."

He closed his eyes for half a second, the words settling deeper than he expected.

"Thank you," he said.

"For what?"

"For not giving up and making space for me."

"Malcolm, you may be the mayor of this town, but I have watched you grow up, you're like one of my own. I would *never* give up on you, and there's always been space for you," she said simply. "You just finally walked into it."

He nodded slowly, the truth hitting him softly.

"Besides, had you not shown up here today, you mama and I were going to knock some sense into you, literally and figuratively." she laughed raising a fist.

Malcolm raised his hands in surrender. "Yes ma'am, I believe you and I'm glad I came to my senses too." he laughed.

As the evening settled and conversations softened, Malcolm found himself breathing differently. He felt anchored in the love he was surrounded with today.

And as he helped gather plates and blow out candles, he looked around at everyone and could, not only see, but *feel* the love that had always been there for him.

This wasn't the end of the healing. But it was the beginning of him choosing to come back to life.

And that was enough for today.

Chapter 12

Monday morning arrived with a faint chill, the kind that hinted winter was only a breath away. Malcolm stepped out onto his porch with a mug of coffee in hand, watching his breath float into the air like small clouds.

The street was quiet, still, and peaceful.

He took a slow sip, letting the warmth roll through him.

After a moment, he grabbed his coat and decided to walk instead of drive. Downtown wasn't far, and something about the crisp morning felt like an invitation to move.

As he made his way along the sidewalk, he noticed things he normally overlooked; the way frost kissed the edges of fallen leaves, the soft clatter of a flag against its pole, the distant murmur of early risers preparing for the workday.

When he reached the square, he paused.

Volunteers were already transforming it—taking down the last Thanksgiving decorations and replacing them with garlands of evergreen, strands of red ribbon, strings of lights waiting to be hung. A ladder leaned against the large oak tree. Boxes labeled *CHRISTMAS MARKET* sat stacked beside the fountain.

The town was shifting seasons.

And for the first time in years...he felt ready to shift with it.

He walked slowly through the square, nodding to the handful of workers who waved as they unpacked ornaments and wreaths.

"Morning, Mayor!" someone called.

He raised his hand in greeting. "Morning."

A group of children hurried past him carrying a plastic tub of ornaments, each one layered in glitter and smudged paint. They giggled as they went, arguing over where the star should go.

Malcolm smiled, a small, genuine curve of his mouth that surprised even him.

As he approached the fountain, he stopped again.Someone had already wrapped the railing in evergreen garland and installed a small nativity scene nearby. The water rippled gently beneath the glow of the early lights.

He felt something soften inside him.

He sat on the stone ledge for a moment, letting the quiet movement of the square surround him. The cold air brushed against his cheeks, carrying with it the scent of pine and early cinnamon bread from the nearby bakery.

A year ago, moments like this would have knocked the wind out of him. Every new season felt like another reminder that she wasn't here, her laughter in the kitchen, the way she fussed over decorations, the quiet little traditions she loved so much. She always said hope mattered, especiallly when life felt a little heavy.

But standing here today, the memory didn't weigh him down. It settled with in him gently, proof that grief could soften, shift and leave room for whatever would come next.

A voice drifted from behind him, friendly, warm and familiar.

"Getting a head start on the season, Mayor?"

He turned to see Mr. Lawrence carrying a tangled mess of lights.

"Looks like the town is," Malcolm replied with a soft laugh.

Lawrence shook his head. "Christmas comes whether we're ready or not. But it's good to see you out here."

"Good to be here," Malcolm said, and this time, he didn't have to force the words.

Lawrence nodded, as though he could hear the truth in them, then walked off to help the others.

Malcolm took one more look around. The garlands. The wreaths. The excited kids. The promise of a new season unfolding piece by piece.

He slipped his hands into his coat pockets and let out a slow, steady breath.

For the first time in a long while, he wasn't standing outside of life looking in.

He was part of it. Still healing, growing and learning how to move forward.

But moving all the same.

As he stood to leave, the sun broke through the clouds, casting a soft, golden light across the square. It illuminated the lanterns, the garlands, the fountain's gleam — and Malcolm felt something stir in his chest.

Something like hope.. Something New.

He turned toward home, a faint smile touching his lips.

Maybe this year...he'd let joy meet him where he was.

And maybe, just maybe, he'd be ready for whatever the next season brought.

THE END....or rather...THE BEGINNING

A
NEW KIND
of
CHRISTMAS
A KINDRED HEARTS STORY
T. LAWREN

Aurora Denver kept her pace steady as she crossed the street, her breath rising in the cold morning air. Boston was already moving, already loud, already in full swing; and usually, she loved that. The noise, the energy, the rush... it felt familiar. It felt like home.

Today, it just felt like something she needed to get through.

She stepped into her office building, shaking off the snow, and glanced down at her phone. The reminder she'd tried to ignore flashed again.

Estate meeting — 10:30 AM.

Her stomach pulled tight.

Aunt Celeste.

She hadn't said the name out loud since the funeral, and she definitely wasn't ready for the meeting that came with it. But she went, because avoiding it wouldn't change anything.

The attorney was kind. Gentle. He walked her through everything slowly. Aurora nodded even though her mind drifted every few seconds. Hearing Celeste reduced to forms and signatures felt wrong.

Then came the condition.

When Aurora stepped back onto the sidewalk, the cold hit her harder than before.

Stay in Eden's Harbour through the holidays.

Live in the cottage.

And if she wanted to inherit it fully...

She had to be married by Valentine's Day.

She stood still for several seconds, letting the traffic and voices blur around her.

Married? By Valentine's Day?! Her thoughts echoed

"Auntie... really?" she whispered.

It sounded like a joke, one Celeste wasn't here to tell her she was just kidding. Aurora wasn't even dating. She barely had time to water the plant in her apartment, let alone consider marriage.

She shoved her hands deeper into her coat pockets and started walking without any real direction. Her brain felt scrambled, trying to fit this strange condition into the life she'd built.

The cottage had meant everything to her when she was younger. It was the one place that felt peaceful, where she followed Celeste around the garden and listened to stories about love and independence and choosing your own life.

Aurora admired that about her aunt, maybe too much. She'd spent her twenties chasing that same independence, forgetting Celeste had also lived with regret she rarely talked about.

Now Aurora had to go back.

She paused at the corner and let out a long breath.

"Okay. I'll go," she said quietly. "I'll get through it."

A quick trip.

Handle the holidays.

Sign whatever needed to be signed.

Figure out the rest later.

That was the plan.

But as she stood there, letting the cold settle around her, something tightened in her chest. She couldn't explain it. Grief, maybe. Annoyance. Confusion. All of it layered together in a way she didn't want to unpack.

Aurora shook her head, pushing the feeling away. She didn't have time to fall apart in the middle of the sidewalk.

She straightened her coat, adjusted her bag, and started walking toward the station.

Boston would still be here when she got back.

Nothing had to change.

A NEW KIND OF THANKSGIVING

At least, that's what she kept telling herself

As always, Thank you God, without you, I wouldn't have this gift to write.

A special thank you to my leaders for your continuous encourage-ment, prayers and love.

And to my daddy. You are forever missed, thank you for showing me so much love that I am able to write that into my characters. Your love lives on through me and through the father figures I create in books.

 T. Lawren is a Southeast Texas native and faith-based author and speaker dedicated to helping others rediscover their identity, reconnect with God, and boldly walk in purpose.

A lifelong lover of reading and writing, she felt the call to publish her first book in her late 30s, reminding others that it's never too late to start something new.

Through her transformative works like *The Path to Purpose* and its Reflection Guide, she encourages readers to embrace healing, spiritual growth, and intentional living, one page at a time. Alongside her nonfiction work, she also writes Christian fiction, weaving stories that offer hope, connection, and faith-filled insight.

Her writing speaks to individuals navigating life's transitions, reminding them that their story still matters.